The Sharing Book

Dianne White

Illustrations by
Simone Shin

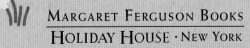
MARGARET FERGUSON BOOKS
HOLIDAY HOUSE · NEW YORK

Sun is perfect for mornings.
Clouds are just right for sky.
Wonder is waiting to happen and . . .

TODAY, this day, is for sharing.

A hand is perfect for holding.
A smile is just right for hello.
A pinkie is waiting to promise and . . .

FRIENDS, best friends, are for sharing.

A plate is perfect for pancakes.
A cup is just right for juice.

A bowl is waiting
for berries and . . .

MEALS, our meals, are for sharing.

A tree is perfect for hiding.
A tire is just right for a swing.

A rope is waiting for climbers and . . .

LAUGHTER, our laughter, is for sharing.

A pole is perfect for fishing.
A canoe is just right for a ride.

A trail is waiting for hikers and . . .

ADVENTURE, this adventure, is for sharing.

A hammock is perfect
for dreaming. A chair
is just right for three.

A lap is waiting for loved ones and . . .

STORIES, our stories, are for sharing.

A stick is perfect for drumming.
A string is just right for a strum.

A song is waiting for voices and . . .

MUSIC, our music, is for sharing.

Moon is perfect for evenings.
Stars are just right for sky.

Two friends are ready for bedtime and . . .

Near or far,
whoever you are . . .

LOVE is for sharing.

For friends—best friends—Steph, Stephanie, Miriam, Nancy, Deb, Candy,
and Ann—for sharing your laughter, adventures, stories, and love —D.W.

For my peaceful, loving, and caring friend, Ash. —S.S.

Margaret Ferguson Books

Text copyright © 2023 by Dianne White

Illustrations copyright © 2023 by Simone Shin

All Rights Reserved

HOLIDAY HOUSE is registered in the U.S. Patent and Trademark Office.

Printed and bound in February 2023 at Leo Paper, Heshan, China.

The artwork for this book is both hand painted and digital.

Book design by Jennifer Browne

www.holidayhouse.com

First Edition

1 3 5 7 9 10 8 6 4 2

Library of Congress Cataloging-in-Publication Data

Names: White, Dianne, author. | Shin, Simone, illustrator.

Title: The sharing book / by Dianne White ; illustrated by Simone Shin.

Description: First edition. | New York : Holiday House, [2023] | "Margaret

Ferguson Books." | Summary: Three families come together and share

everything from juice to joy on a camping trip.

Identifiers: LCCN 2022018040 | ISBN 9780823443475 (hardcover)

Subjects: CYAC: Sharing—Fiction. | Camping—Fiction. | Families—Fiction.

Classification: LCC PZ7.1.W4426 Sh 2023 | DDC [E]—dc23

LC record available at https://lccn.loc.gov/2022018040

ISBN: 978-0-8234-4347-5 (hardcover)